COMPROMISED BRIDE VIRGINIA

Compromised Brides series

Cheryl Wright

Copyright

Virginia
(Compromised Brides series)

Copyright ©2022 by Cheryl Wright

Small Town Romance Publications

Cover Artist: Silver Sage Book Covers

All rights reserved. Without limiting the rights under copyright reserved above, no part of this publication may be reproduced, stored in or introduced into a retrieval system, or transmitted, in any form, or by any means (electronic, mechanical, photocopying, recording, or otherwise) without the prior written permission of the copyright owner of this book.

This is a work of fiction. Characters, places, and incidents are a figment of the author's imagination. Any resemblance to actual events, locales, organizations or people living or dead, is totally coincidental.

This book was written by a human and not Artificial Intelligence (A.I.).

This book can not be used to train Artificial Intelligence (A.I.).

Dedication

To Margaret Tanner, my very dear friend and fellow author, for her enduring encouragement and friendship.

To Alan, my husband of over forty-nine years, who has been a relentless supporter of my writing and dreams for many years.

To You, my wonderful readers, who encourage me to continue writing these stories. It is such a joy knowing so many of you enjoy reading my stories as much as I love writing them for you.

Table of Contents

Copyright 2
Dedication 3
Table of Contents 4
Chapter One 5
Chapter Two 14
Chapter Three 27
Chapter Four 35
Chapter Five 46
Chapter Six 56
Chapter Seven 67
Chapter Eight.. 77
Chapter Nine 89
Chapter Ten 98
Epilogue 106
From the Author 112
About the Author.. 113
Links... 114

Virginia

Chapter One

Billings, Montana, late 1880's

Virginia Black pulled her cloak up around herself.

She felt both excitement and trepidation about what lay ahead. This was her very first assignment as a governess, and she was certain it was just the beginning of a wonderful life.

She stared at the profile of her employer, Mr. Bartholomew Llewellyn.

"We have arrived," he said, climbing down from the buggy. "I'm sorry you've had to endure such a dreary trip. Let's hope the weather is better tomorrow." He smiled tentatively, then glanced at the overcast sky.

He busied himself with pulling her meagre luggage from the buggy, then headed to the front door. Virginia shivered at the prospect of living in this house, this mansion. From the outside, it seemed lifeless. Through the windows, despite the curtains being drawn, it appeared to be in darkness.

Mr. Llewellyn assured her during their long trip, his wife and children would have returned before they arrived.

He rattled the door handle, then let out a low growl. He turned to face her. "Forgive me. It appears my wife hasn't yet arrived, and it's the housekeeper's day off." His annoyance was evident as he pulled a key from his pocket.

Pushing the door wide, he ushered her through, then followed behind and brought her luggage inside. Lighting a lantern, he waved her ahead and up the stairs. In the near darkness, Virginia had a feeling of foreboding, but knew it was her imagination getting the better of her.

"Your room is to the left," he said, his voice echoing in the empty house. "The nursery is next door – they're adjoining rooms. Katherine, when she arrives, will go through all the details. In the meantime, settle yourself in, then come down to the kitchen. I'll put the kettle on." He opened the bedroom door and ushered her inside, dropping her small suitcase just inside the room. And then he was gone.

Virginia glanced around the room. It wasn't huge, but it wasn't tiny either. There was a single bed, which was adorned by a colorful quilt, a bedside cupboard with three drawers. A comfortable chair sat in the corner. Atop the cupboard sat a lantern and a bible.

She walked over to the window and stared out. Not that she could see much in the near darkness, but

Virginia

Virginia could make out a large garden at the back of the house. On either side, there appeared to be houses, but she couldn't be sure.

When she'd arrived, Virginia had noticed houses on the opposite side of the road, but none close to the size of her employer's home. From what she understood, Bartholomew Llewellyn was a banker, and a high profile one at that. He had a standing in the community that couldn't be equaled. It was the reason she was so nervous about taking this job, but she had little choice. She either accepted this posting, or forgot about becoming a governess for the high-class agency she'd enrolled with. Refusing two previous positions because of their remote locations, this was her last opportunity. If she didn't take this listing, they were going to ban her from any future work through them.

Virginia neither wanted, nor could afford to have them do that. Father had given her an ultimatum: take the position, or find somewhere else to live. According to him, she was far too old to be living at home, and at twenty-three, well past a respectable age to marry.

Except she didn't want to marry. Especially since Father tried to pair her with whomever took his whim. Most of the *gentlemen* he'd chosen were little more than storekeepers. Virginia foresaw a better life for herself. Her family was not wealthy, far from it, but they weren't poor either. She didn't see herself living a life of luxury with the person she eventually married, but she didn't want to live in a hovel, either.

She unpacked the little luggage she possessed and placed it in the drawers. She then went downstairs to the kitchen. Mr. Llewellyn had promised tea, and she was parched. She was looking forward to the hot beverage. The trip from the train station was cold, and she was close to shivering by the time they arrived.

"Ah, there you are, my dear." Mr. Llewellyn placed a mug of tea on the table for her. "You look chilled to the bone. Take your tea and warm yourself up by the fire." He was quite fatherly, she thought, beginning to feel comfortable around him. She couldn't wait to meet his wife, and craned her neck to glance through to the next room. "I'm afraid my wife hasn't arrived yet," he said with a sigh. "She should have been here hours ago, along with your young charges." He smiled then, and Virginia felt even more relaxed than she had already.

"Thank you. I can't wait to meet them all." She took a sip of the tea. Warmth flooded her as it slid down her throat. It was already doing its job, and she continued to drink as she sat by the fire, her employer sitting opposite.

"Perhaps we should rustle up something to eat," he said out of the blue. "I assume you haven't eaten?"

Virginia

She shook her head. Time had got away with her, and the last thing Virginia had expected was the length of the trip from the station to her new home.

He rummaged through the kitchen cupboards, but came up with nothing. "Do you have a pantry?"

He stared at her, dumbfounded. "I do not know. The housekeeper manages all that."

Glancing about, Virginia spotted what might be a pantry, and checked it out. "Would you like pancakes?" she called to him, and was greeted with a resounding yes. He made small talk while she cooked, asking about her family, where she was from, and many other questions she didn't expect. It wasn't that he was being nosey, he was trying to fill in the empty space. She fully understood that. She simply hadn't expected to be bombarded with personal questions.

"They're ready," she could finally say, and waved for him to sit down. She placed a plate in the center of the table and waited for him to take his fill first.

"Eat up," he said. "Don't wait for me. Otherwise you might miss out." He smiled then. If he hadn't, she might not have known he was teasing her.

After supper was over, she cleaned up the kitchen, and bid her new employer goodnight. She was exhausted and needed to sleep. Virginia was excited to meet her employer's wife when she woke in the morning.

Virginia awoke with a start. She glanced about, trying to get her bearings, but had no idea where she was. It didn't take long for her to recall once she was fully awake. She climbed out of bed and went straight to the window. Last night she'd longed to see the garden, now was her chance.

She stared through the window – what a beautiful view. It was far better than the view from her own bedroom back home. As the sun rose over the hills, the pink and blue of the sky sent the feeling of peacefulness through her. It was probably the last time today that would happen. Once the children were awake, she would surely be on her toes. She hadn't met them yet, but at their young ages, she couldn't imagine they would be easy to control.

Finally fully awake, Virginia quickly dressed, then tiptoed to the next room to peek in on her new charges. She quietly opened the door; shock punched the breath from her lungs. The room was empty, and the beds hadn't been slept in.

Reality hit her with a thud. She'd spent the night alone in this big house with only her employer. Horror bubbled up inside her – but then sanity settled in. She must be mistaken. The children must have spent the night with their parents. Mr.

Virginia

Llewellyn surely wouldn't put her reputation at risk by allowing her to stay alone in the house with him?

Her heart pounded. Last night, he assured her his wife and children would return. She slowly made her way downstairs, heading toward the kitchen. She would make herself a cup of tea and force herself to think more rationally. The soft humming alerted her to the housekeeper milling about in the busiest room of the house.

"Good morning," she said, and the other woman jumped.

"Oh, my Lord! You did startle me," she said, putting a hand to her chest. "Luckily I wasn't 'oldin a sharp knife. Martha Simpson, housekeeper. You must be Miss Virginia." The housekeeper smiled briefly, then handed her a mug of hot tea.

Virginia nodded. "What time did Mrs. Llewellyn and the children arrive last night?"

"Oh, I don't live 'ere. I come in days. You'll 'ave to ask the mister." They both turned at the sound of footfalls on the stairs.

"Good morning Mr. Llewellyn. I wondered what time your family arrived last night." Virginia felt unsure of even asking, but wouldn't feel comfortable until she knew.

He tugged at his tie. "I'm afraid she didn't. I can only think they must have been caught up with the snow." A brief smile tugged at his lips, but Virginia stared.

Martha stared.

Her employer went red.

"I know it's not ideal, but it couldn't be avoided." He sat down at the table then, and Martha placed a mug of coffee in front of him.

"I don't want t' speak out of turn, Sir, but this could compromise the governess." Martha wore a frown that threatened Virginia's peace of mind.

"I'm not…" Virginia suddenly clamped her mouth shut. Martha was right, she had been compromised.

"I won't tell if you don't," he said flippantly. "No one else is aware, so it will be our secret." He winked then, and Virginia watched as fury boiled across Martha's face.

"If you don't mind me saying so, Sir, it don't work that way." She grabbed a kitchen towel and dried her hands, then sat at the table, facing her employer. "I'm sorry t' say, yer don't understand how it works. Sir," she added. Virginia was aware the older woman was risking her job for her, a complete stranger. It tugged at her heart. "Once yer reputation is sullied, ain't no way t' get it back."

Virginia sat speechless. Her worst fears had been realized – she'd spent the night alone with her

Virginia

employer, and there was nothing she could do to remedy the situation.

He suddenly stood, sending his chair flying across the room. "We won't speak of this again," he bellowed. "It was unintentional, and nothing happened. Miss Black went to bed around seven, and I didn't see her again until now."

"That's true," Virginia said, her voice small. She couldn't lose this job, she absolutely couldn't. It was her last chance with the agency. If the Llewellyn's sent her away, she'd be in a dire situation. What she would do, she had absolutely no idea. Whatever it was, she knew it wouldn't be easy. With her reputation in tatters, no one would employ her as a governess. This position was supposed to resolve all her problems and her worries. *What would she do if Mr. Llewellyn sent her away?*

On the other hand, how could she stay here now?

Chapter Two

The last thing Virginia would do was go home begging to her father after Mrs. Llewellyn told her to leave after finally arriving home.

Once she'd explained the situation to the agency who placed her as a governess, they wiped their hands of her. It was an immense disappointment, since she was only in this dire situation because of them.

Clutching the few belongings she possessed, Virginia decided her only option was to find some other type of work. She possessed few skills that would land her a job, but she could only try. Her next challenge was where to find that work. To that end, she purchased a newspaper. It hurt spending the little money she had, and she would have to be diligent to get through until work presented itself.

Reaching into her reticule, Virginia came across an envelope given to her by Bartholomew Llewellyn. He was as upset about the situation as her. It was obvious his wife ruled the roost when it came to domestic matters. He had handed her the letter sized envelope as he left her at the station. With the train arriving shortly afterwards, she had no time to check it out.

Virginia

She opened the newspaper, since her need for work was more important than reading a fictitious recommendation, assuming that's what he'd given her, and she scrolled down the advertisements. Virginia was not a qualified cook, she had no experience as a nurse, and she most certainly wasn't a mechanic. She stared at the newspaper in dismay. Her life was in tatters and at this very moment, she was homeless. Her only option was to return home with her tail between her legs. It was a last resort.

Disheartened, she folded the newspaper and laid it on her lap. Then she pulled the envelope out of her reticule and began to open it. The moment the flap opened, she saw it – enough money to keep her going for at least two weeks, if not more. She quickly shoved the envelope back into her reticule. The last thing she needed was to advertise she was carrying a large quantity of money.

As much as she felt bad, Mr. Llewellyn had paid her a stipend despite her not working for him, she was grateful he did. Now she would have enough money to get her through for the next couple of weeks until she found a paying position. She sighed with relief. But she also felt quite emotional. She wished she'd known what he'd given her. That way, she could have thanked him in person.

On the other hand, she might have denied his generosity, and that would have been foolish, given the circumstances.

Virginia swallowed back the emotion that threatened to overtake her. She would not cry. Especially since she sat on the train, surrounded by several people, all of whom appeared to be staring at her. Surely she imagined it?

To take her mind off her situation, Virginia continued to study the newspaper. Hmmm, study might be too strong a word, she decided. The printed words swirled across the page, and she found it difficult to read them. She snapped the pages closed and sat with her back straight, her head held high.

The constant movement of the train lulled her into a deep sleep, until she found herself thrown to the floor, landing on top of her newspaper, which was now spread about.

"My goodness! Are you all right, Miss?" Strong arms helped Virginia to her feet, then gathered up the newspaper she'd had sitting on her lap. It was the perfect end to the most horrific time in her life.

The shame she felt was overwhelming. Virginia had done nothing wrong, but she was the one who'd been sent away, and the one who'd lost her job. She could never tell her friends or her family. She would be ridiculed and denigrated for the rest of her life. No, this was something that had to remain hidden, otherwise she would never get a job, even one of the lowest standard. And she most certainly would never marry. Any man worth marrying would presume she had truly been desecrated in the most awful of ways.

She dared to glance up. The man had the most beautiful smile, and instead of feeling warmed by it, she turned away. Never again would she be able to face anyone. Men especially. Despite being totally innocent, she was the one being punished. Her heart pounded.

"Miss? Can I do something to help you?" She glanced at him again. He seemed genuinely concerned about her. Instead of waiting for an answer, he guided her into her seat, then sat beside her.

If only he knew her deepest, darkest secret, and what it would mean to any man who dared take any interest in her. "I.. I'm fine. Thank you." If she could curl up and die right now, it would be the best for all concerned. Especially Virginia.

He frowned. "You are clearly not fine." He stared at her then, concern written all over his face. "What can I do to help?"

It was the first time she could ever recall anyone taking an interest in her. Worrying about her. It felt good, but she also didn't know what to do about it, especially given her new status as a compromised woman.

She shook her head. She'd had enough of this conversation. It was making her feel emotional, and Virginia didn't want that. Despite her best efforts, tears welled up in her eyes. She turned her face away from the stranger, trying to hide her dismay.

"Next stop, Shady Hollow," the conductor called as he strolled through the carriage.

"Is this your stop?" the stranger asked. Virginia had no idea, simply because she had no plan of where she was going. Perhaps she would alight here and continue to another town later if this one didn't appeal.

"It is," she said firmly, and gathered up her overnight bag and her reticule. It embarrassed her that these were her only possessions.

The moment the train stopped moving, the stranger was on his feet. "Do you have to be somewhere anytime soon?" He looked hopeful, and Virginia had nothing else to do at the moment, so why not see what he had to say?

"Nothing right now," she said, throwing him a tentative smile.

In return, he beamed. "There's a small café close to here if you'd care to join me." *Should she?* After all, she didn't have a lot of money to spare, and it might mean missing out on a meal at some point. "My

Virginia

treat," he added. *How could she resist an offer like that?*

"I'd love to!" She blurted the words out before she could stop herself, then instantly regretted it. The last thing Virginia wanted was to give the wrong impression. She wasn't sure if this young man was interested in her, or simply being friendly. Already she appeared over-eager.

He hooked his arm through hers and guided Virginia toward the café. They left the train station, and he took her out onto the main street. She spotted a café, but he didn't take her there. "Isn't that the café?" she asked, feeling confused.

"There's a far better one further up and around the corner," he said cheerfully, and she reveled in his wonderful smile.

The more they walked, the more concerned she became. The main street was now well behind them, and the buildings were sparse this far from town. She tugged her arm, trying to pull it free, but his grip became intense and she couldn't break away.

And then they turned the corner. Virginia's heart thudded. There was no café on this street. In fact, there was nothing. It was a dark back lot, overshadowed by disintegrating buildings. She again struggled to pull free, to no avail. She wanted to run, needed to run, but he held her in a tight grip.

The stranger grinned.

Virginia tried not to cower, but it was hard not to. "Give me your reticule and I'll be on my way," he said with a sneer. This man was the complete opposite of the one she'd met on the train. He was not nice, and he certainly wasn't helpful. He only wanted to rob her.

"I thought you were a gentleman," she near snarled, trying not to let her emotions rule her.

He sneered again. "Well, you thought wrong," he said, dragging her reticule from her. "I only want that envelope. You can have the rest."

Her eyes opened wide with astonishment. *He'd seen what was in the envelope?* What a fool she'd been. Especially not knowing what was enclosed. She'd been an idiot to take it out in public. Now she was going to pay the price.

Taking a deep breath, she let it out slowly. He had her cornered.

She glanced about. There was no where to run. No chance to get away. Virginia opened her reticule and was about to hand the wad of money over when she heard a noise behind her.

Today surely couldn't get any worse.

"Don't move or I'll shoot."

Virginia

Virginia heard her own intake of breath. *Was the thief now being robbed?* She was petrified, and it was all she could do not to fall in a heap on the ground.

The stranger let his hands drop to his sides. "Turn around slowly and put your hands up. Miss, you come here." Virginia did not know how she put one foot in front of the other, but she did. The moment she was near the handsome stranger who held a gun on the horrible man from the train, he pushed her behind him. She was tempted to run. But would her legs carry her?

Then she noticed another man turn the corner. She couldn't take much more.

The sun glinted off something on the newcomer's chest. She wasn't sure what to think. Did she have two robbers and a deputy, or two deputies and a robber? It was all too much and her head was spinning.

"I will not tell you again. Turn around." The last words were ground out, but Walt Riley knew he had to keep calm. He'd been after this fool for far too long, and it was only perchance he'd spotted the young woman being guided toward this empty back lot. He knew in his gut he'd found his robber. The man turned, and Walt roughly handcuffed him.

Only then was he ready to turn and check on the woman. "Miss, are you all right?"

She nodded, but it was obvious she was far from fine. Tears danced on the edge of her eyelashes. It was as though she dared them not to fall. She was a stranger to town, probably lured here by the man standing in front of him. "What is your name?" he asked gently. She appeared to be in shock, and given the circumstances, he couldn't blame her.

"Virginia." She swallowed then. "Virginia Black." Her voice broke, and she swiped at the tears that slid down her cheeks.

He waved toward his deputy, who took control of their prisoner, and headed toward the jail. Walt offered her his hand. "Marshal Walton Riley," he said firmly, hoping to reassure her. It didn't seem to work. Her whole body was shaking, and who could blame her? The man he'd arrested only moments ago was violent. Numerous other women had been assaulted for mere dollars. One had been left for dead, but thankfully pulled through.

He put a hand to her back and guided the victim toward the jail. He needed a statement from her. In the meantime, a little small talk might calm her down. "Where are you from, Miss Black?" The question seemed to confuse her.

"I was traveling from…" She stared up at him with big brown eyes and shook her head. "The position I went there for turned out badly." Her bottom lip quivered, and he decided to divert her attention away from that line of questioning.

"How did you get caught up with that fool?" So far, Walt didn't know who he was dealing with. He guessed the man had lived in the shadows for years. This was not something his predecessor had warned him about.

"The train jolted, and I fell to the floor. He helped me." She glanced up at him again, those brown eyes dancing with fear at the memory of it.

He reached out and put his arm through hers. It was not something he would normally do, particularly with a victim, but it was apparent she was traumatized. She stared at their linked arms. Not horrified, which he thought might be the case, but she seemed to be reassured. He'd hoped that would be the outcome.

Then he did something he had no intention of doing. He patted her hand.

That simple action had her face softening. The terror seemed to drop away, and the shaking stopped. Her once pale face had color in it again. For a minute there, he thought he'd have to call the doc, but now, he was convinced she would be all right.

He opened the door to the Marshal's Office and indicated for her to sit down. The deputy entered the room and placed a key in the top drawer of the desk. "He's locked up, and not saying a word. Won't give up his name either."

Walt grunted. He expected nothing less. "You are safe now, Miss Black." He stared at her, trying to decide how much information to give away. She seemed settled now, and he plowed on. "Did he steal anything from you?"

She shook her head. "You stopped him."

He frowned. It occurred to him their prisoner had only targeted women with sizeable sums of cash, but he did not know how he knew what they were carrying. "Do you know how he knew you had a lot of money on you?" He stopped then. "Presuming you did."

"I did. My new employer paid a severance, but I didn't realize. He'd put it in an envelope and I… I thought it was a reference."

"And you opened it on the train."

She paled again, but Walt wasn't sure why. At least he knew why this woman was targeted. "This will be difficult to hear," he said gently. "But you were lucky. The other women were beaten. One woman was left for dead."

Virginia

She swayed in her seat, and he was certain she was going to faint. It was too much. He shouldn't have told her. Especially this soon.

He hurried around to her. "Get the doc," he ordered his deputy, as he held her firmly. Too late, after his deputy had left, he realized he should have taken her to the doc, not the other way around.

"I'm fine, I promise," she said, but she didn't seem fine.

Walt brought her a glass of water and watched her sip it. He'd been loathe to leave her side, but surely it wouldn't hurt to give her water? Doc arrived in no time, but she still insisted she was all right. "Let me be the judge of that," Doc told her, and she pursed her lips. Walt could see the rebel in her kicking in. It was a pity she hadn't thought that way when their prisoner had enticed her to go with him.

"It's shock," Doc said, then turned to his patient. "I'd like you to come back to my surgery so I can check you over properly. You can rest there as well."

She defiantly shook her head. "I'm fine, I promise," she said. "Are you finished with me, Marshal?"

He stared at her momentarily. She sure was adamant not to admit how upset she was. "For now. I'll need a statement, and I'll need you to testify when the judge arrives. That could be a week, two weeks, or even longer." He shrugged. The judge arrived when it suited him.

She was aghast. "I hadn't planned on staying."

"We'll put you up for the duration. You won't be out of pocket," Walt said. She nodded, and he understood by that simple gesture she was worried about the cost. "I'll make all the arrangements while you are checked out." This time he didn't ask. He stated the facts. Doing that meant she had no chance to argue.

At least he hoped she wouldn't.

Virginia

Chapter Three

Virginia couldn't believe her luck. Or lack thereof.

In the past two days, she'd begun a new job – one that was meant to last several years. She'd been compromised, then she'd almost been assaulted. Praise the Lord she'd been rescued. And by a handsome marshal, no less.

She knew she shouldn't, but how could a gal not admire such a man? Apart from being so good looking, he'd saved her from that… monster.

She shivered.

If he'd arrived only moments later, it could have been a totally different story. If what the marshal said was true, and she had no reason not to believe him, her attacker was violent. He'd already assaulted several women. All for the sake of robbing them. The thought was enough to make her cry.

But she refused to let that happen. She'd done plenty of that when she'd lost her job over the situation back at the Llewellyn's. It was not her fault, and yet she was the one who had to pay the price. At least Mr. Llewellyn had been generous with covering her wages for the next two weeks.

With everything that had happened, she still hadn't counted the money he'd given her.

The position, had it lasted, included board and replenishing her wardrobe to ensure she fulfilled the expectations as the Llewellyn's governess. She'd lost a lot, but more than anything, she'd lost her reputation.

If the housekeeper had promised not to say anything, things would have been different, but the woman had mentioned it to Mrs. Llewellyn who had turned on her, screaming that Virginia had tried to seduce her husband. When Virginia left, it was doubtful the housekeeper would still have a job when Mr. Llewellyn returned from dropping her at the station. He certainly hadn't looked pleased at the housekeeper's behavior in complaining to his wife.

Virginia was in the depth of despair. Her life had been turned upside down in literally two days. She could only imagine what her father would think. Knowing the way he felt about her recently, he would put all the blame on her, despite none of it being her doing. She was the innocent victim of circumstances.

The worst part was she didn't even get to meet the children. As she'd left the house, she stared at the family photograph standing proudly in the entrance hall. They were adorable. It pained her even more

Virginia

when she saw that photograph. Virginia knew she would have been happy living and working there.

It was water under the bridge now. That was in the past, and she had to look to the future. Her future was not in Shady Hollow – the name of the town should have been a warning. A precursor to the bleakness that was ahead of her.

She chuckled at the way her thoughts were going. "Are you all right, Miss Black?" Doc's friendly face was hovering above her.

"I am. I was thinking about the name of this town, and how it had turned out to be an omen."

He shook his head. "You didn't have much of a welcoming, did you now? Let me assure you, others here are decent people. You were unlucky to meet the only one who wasn't." She tried to sit up, and he took her hand to assist. "Take the marshal, for example. He's as honest as they come. Do anything for anyone."

She knew that first hand. He was arranging accommodation for her at that very moment. "I wonder if he's found anywhere for me to stay."

"There's always rooms available in Shady Hollow. It's not the sort of place that gets booked out. It's a quiet town. People come here and never leave."

Except Virginia knew she would leave. She had no choice but to wait until after the man's trial, but then she'd be gone. Where her destination might be, she had no idea, but she would think about it and come up with a plan. One thing was certain: she wouldn't return home to her father and his authoritarian ways.

The door suddenly flew open. She gasped. A hand touched her shoulder – she'd not known such gentleness for quite some time. Probably since her mother had died. Doc looked annoyed. "You gave the young lady quite a fright, Marshal." He frowned then, and Marshal Riley appeared startled.

"Apologies, Miss Black. I didn't think."

"I'm fine," she said, knowing full well that wasn't the case. *Why did she always put on a front?* Pretending she was fine when she wasn't was a learned behavior. She'd been doing it for years. If she said she wasn't fine, Father would bellow that she was. Oh, he was the perfect father in company, but when it was only the two of them, it was a different story altogether.

"She's not fine," Doc said firmly. "Miss Black is quivering again." He glared at the marshal.

His face dropped. "I am truly sorry, Miss Black. On a happier note, I have secured accommodation for you. It's at the ladies' boarding house."

"It's quite lovely there," Doc said, and she believed him. "Annie Miller will look after you. She's an excellent cook, too."

Virginia

"Doc should know," the marshal said. He winked at her then, and Virginia wasn't sure what that was about.

"If you feel up to it, I can take you there now." He handed Virginia her reticule, and she stared at it. She hadn't realized it was even out of her possession. She agreed, and they left the doctor's surgery.

"I'm worried about you carrying that amount of money around, and locked the envelope in the safe. I don't think you realize how much you had on you. Or what you had to lose if our John Doe had robbed you."

Her eyes opened wide in astonishment. "There is at least two month's wages there," he said quietly, ensuring he wasn't overheard. "Unless you spend it all at once, you could call yourself very well off." He glanced down at her then. "Who exactly were you meant to work for?"

She swallowed. Virginia had no intention of telling him all the gory details. "A banker."

"Well," Marshal Riley said. "That makes sense. They have plenty of money," he said, then chuckled at his own words.

But Virginia didn't chuckle. She didn't even smile. Knowing what that man had done to her, to her plans, to her reputation, it made her furious.

"Is everything all right? You look none too pleased." He pushed his hat back and scratched his head. "Was it something I said?" He looked truly confused.

"No. I promise. It wasn't you, it was the banker." She prayed he wouldn't ask any more questions. Right now, the last thing she wanted was to confess she was a tainted woman who knew she would never be able to marry, and knew no man would ever want to marry her, anyway. She swallowed. Hard. It was a hard realization, but the sooner she understood the truth of her situation, the better. She could never get close to any man, never wed, and certainly would never have children. Her heart thudded, and pain shot through her. She stumbled at the terrible realization of her forced situation.

Strong hands reached for her and pulled her against him, trying to steady her. The marshal guided her to a nearby bench. "I think I should take you back to the doc." He studied her, his worry apparent.

Virginia shook her head vigorously. "Please, no! I promise I'm fine." There she went again, telling lies, covering up her true feelings. She stared up at him. "The truth is, I'm not fine. I feel more than a little overwhelmed at what occurred today." She studied her hands twisting in her lap.

"That's understandable," he said quietly. "Hopefully, it will all be over soon. The judge

Virginia

should be here early next week, and then you can be on your way."

Relief overwhelmed her, and Virginia breathed a long sigh of relief. How she ever got herself into this situation, she would never know. Except she did know. It was her own stupidity at opening the envelope in public view. She should have realized a banker, of all people, wouldn't allow her to lose money because of him. If word got around, he'd be a laughingstock. Or he'd be admonished by his peers and lose his standing in the community. He couldn't risk such a thing, so he'd bought her silence with the money.

She would never do such a ridiculous thing again. She almost laughed. More likely than not, she wouldn't get the chance. If word got out she had been compromised… Virginia wanted to curl up into a ball and cry. It would let out all her pent-up feelings, and might even exorcise her of these feelings of hatred she was experiencing.

Maybe not hate, but if the Llewellyn's housekeeper hadn't forced the situation, she would still have a job. She would be safe in their mansion, and would be caring for those beautiful children. She would be happy instead of experiencing the terror she'd felt just hours ago.

Virginia knew she should instead feel grateful. According to the marshal, she had more money than she'd ever possessed. In fact, more than she'd even seen. It could set her up for life. But where would that life be located? She honestly did not know, and right now her brain hurt and she needed to rest.

"I'm…" She was about to say fine, but stopped herself. Father was not here to bully her, and Virginia needed to be truthful with people. "I'm feeling better," she said instead. The marshal helped her to her feet, and a shiver went down her spine. The surprise on his face showed he might have felt it, too.

She should leave the moment she gave her testimony to the judge. She couldn't get mixed up with any man, let alone one as handsome as this one.

Virginia

Chapter Four

"Miss Annie Miller has owned the ladies' boarding house for a very long time. Far longer than I've been in Shady Hollow. Most of the locals will tell you she's always been here, but she wasn't the original owner – her spinster aunt was." He glanced down at her then, and something shifted. Never before in her life had Virginia felt anything like she did when she was around the marshal. It was utterly crazy. She'd met him earlier today under the most stressful of circumstances. Even now, she still felt quite out of sorts.

They stopped outside a quaint double-storey building. There was a cast-iron fence at the front, and a well-kept garden on either side of the steps. It was lovely, to say the least. Virginia glanced up and noticed the pretty curtains that adorned each window. If the outside was any indication, she would feel right at home.

To be honest, probably more at home than she did at her father's house. She hadn't felt comfortable there for many years. When Mother died, everything changed. Father turned into a completely different person. He no longer treated his only child with the dignity and respect he previously had, and the minute she reached marrying age, tried to push her onto someone else.

He had several young men visit, his plan to get at least one interested enough to court and then wed his daughter. But Virginia was having none of it. When she married, it would be for love, despite what Father said.

It was only one reason she wouldn't return home. The marshal unlatched the gate and waved her through. A woman a little older than Virginia came to the door, and she immediately felt more relaxed. "Welcome, welcome! Do come in. You too, Marshal. I have coffee ready to pour, and a pound cake ready to eat." She smiled and all Virginia's worries seemed to melt away.

"This is Miss Virginia Black. As I explained earlier, she needs a room until the judge hears her testimony."

Miss Miller stepped toward her and wrapped her arms around the younger woman. "You poor dear. I can't begin to imagine what you endured." She rubbed circles over Virginia's back before stepping away. "I have our best room picked out for you. It's at the top of the stairs, and you have the most wonderful view of our lovely town." As they stepped inside, Virginia spotted her belongings sitting at the side of the stairs. "Of course, if you don't like that room, there are plenty more to choose

Virginia

from. It's very quiet at the moment. There are only a few other ladies here." Virginia nodded, not sure what she should say.

She followed Miss Miller up the narrow stairs, and was guided into the first room she saw. Her hostess stood aside, not saying another word. *Perhaps allowing Virginia to make her own decision about the room?* Not that she cared. She was only here because she was given no option. Not once did Marshal Riley tell her she could leave town. It was all about staying to testify.

If she was truthful, Virginia was petrified. *What if she gave her testimony, and the judge set the man free? She shuddered.* "Are you all right, my dear?"

Virginia opened her mouth to speak the false words she always spoke, then changed her mind. "I'm worried the judge will set that man free, and he'll come after me."

It had been a stressful day, but Virginia had found no excuse for the tears that tried to escape several times already today. She closed her eyes, and a tear trickled down her face. She swiped at them, then turned away, trying to hide her embarrassment.

"We're all friends here, my dear. No need to hide your tears." Gentle hands circled her back again, and she felt far more calm. "Look at this wonderful view." She smiled and guided Virginia to the window.

"It is quite beautiful. I could stand here all day." Virginia went over to the bed and sat on the side. It felt comfortable, inviting. The pretty pink curtains matched the meticulously made quilt that sat on the bed. "I adore this room," she said, surprising even herself. Virginia felt so comfortable in here. It was like she'd come home, but with her mother there again. Miss Miller seemed to have a calming effect on her, which was most welcome.

Her hostess called for the marshal to bring up her belongings, and he did as instructed. There was little for him to carry, so she didn't feel the guilt she probably would have if she'd had a heavy trunk. Virginia was handed a key to her room, and Miss Miller stepped into the hallway.

"You must come and meet everyone," her hostess said before going down the stairs.

Virginia pulled the door closed behind her, taking a huge breath and let it out slowly. Marshal Riley was right behind her, and his presence filled her with warmth. She suddenly gasped. The last time she let her guard down she'd been attacked and almost assaulted. Of course, if the marshal hadn't come along when he did, she would probably be laying in her own blood right now.

The man had saved her life. Of course, he was trustworthy.

Virginia

She would keep telling herself that, because right now, she didn't feel as though she could trust anyone. In a span of less than two days, two different men had let her down. Virginia knew in her heart the marshal was not like that, but her head told her she had to be careful and not lower her guard. Her head also told her she would pay the price for trusting anyone.

After all, she'd already done that – twice. Even her own father couldn't be trusted. *What made her think any man was dependable?*

"Here we are," Miss Miller said. "These are the other ladies staying here — Miss Ginny Withers, Miss Mabel Carruthers, and Miss Caroline Jacobson." She pointed to each woman as she said their name. They all smiled and gave her a welcoming nod. "You all know the marshal," she said, then indicated for them both to sit.

She placed a mug of coffee in front of the marshal, and tea for Virginia, telling them to help themselves to cake. "You know I don't have to be told twice," Walt said as he grinned. "Miss Miller is an excellent cook, as I've already told you."

Virginia glanced around the table. Everyone seemed to be friendly, but she would reserve her opinion until she knew them better. She would only be here a few days, so that was highly unlikely to happen. "Thank you," she said, her voice quiet as a church mouse. All eyes turned to her. Were they judging her for the only two words she'd spoken, or did her quiet voice take them off guard? She would probably never know, but she would assume the latter.

"How long are you staying?" Miss Withers asked.

"Only until the judge arrives." All eyes turned to her then.

"Judge?" Miss Carruthers asked. "Are you in some sort of trouble?" She knew the slightly older woman meant well, but wasn't sure she wanted to talk about it just yet.

The marshal glanced at her and she nodded. He spoke on her behalf. "Miss Black was the victim of an attempted robbery. She needs to testify before the judge."

"Oh, you poor dear," Miss Jacobson said, her face softening at the declaration.

"It was rather horrible," Virginia said, preferring not to think about it.

Miss Carruthers sat quietly and didn't utter a word for close to a minute. "I presume I will still have to testify?" she finally asked. Her words confused Virginia.

"It would certainly help." Marshal Riley turned to Virginia then. "Miss Carruthers was also a victim of your robber."

Virginia felt herself pale. How many women had that terrible man robbed? "You were far from his first victim, but depending on the testimonies and the judge, hopefully his last."

He was right. She had to ensure her testimony was strong enough. *Voicing her experience was crucial, but could she do it?* Miss Carruthers studied her. "It's going to be difficult for us both, but we have to ensure he is stopped."

"Of course," she said firmly. *But was her resolve as strong as she sounded right now?* That was yet to be seen.

~*~

When the food was gone and their mugs empty, everyone dispersed. "I think I'll go for a stroll," Virginia said, stretching her arms above her head. She felt the eyes of the marshal on her.

"Would you like company?" he asked. "You've been through a lot, and well, I'd like to ensure you are all right."

She studied him briefly. "Well, thank you, Marshal. That would be lovely." If she was truthful with herself, Virginia was rather reluctant to go out alone. She hoped the feeling would pass sooner than later.

"Walt, please," he said. "It gets to the point I feel like my name is Marshal, and not Walt." He chuckled then, and the sound reverberated through her as warmth flooded her entire being. She smiled, but not too broadly. The last thing she wanted was to let him think she was interested, because she wasn't. She absolutely wasn't.

He linked his arm through hers and headed toward the door. "I should probably get my coat," she said, glancing down at the almost thread-bare gown she wore. Such a pity she'd lost her governess position – it promised to be very worthwhile in many ways.

But the past was the past, and there was absolutely nothing she could do about it.

Walt glanced out the window. "There are a few flurries, so perhaps that is a good idea. He snatched his own coat from the hall stand and shrugged it on as she climbed the stairs.

Entering her room, Virginia paused. Should she even be doing this? She'd already deemed all men to be untrustworthy, so why go? Then again, she'd already agreed, so it was too late to back out now. Besides, she did like Walt, but only as a friend.

He watched her every move as she climbed down the stairs, careful not to slip. It would be far too

Virginia

embarrassing if that happened. Her embarrassment level was already far too high for today. Virginia still couldn't believe she'd put herself in such a dangerous situation. She swallowed down the pain and the emotion of what that man did to her. Worst of all, what he could have done to her. From what she'd been told, she'd had a lucky escape.

Walt Riley had saved her, and yet here she was admonishing the man. And for absolutely no reason.

He reached out and took her hand as she took the last two steps. His skin was soft and warm and dwarfed her tiny hands in comparison. She hadn't noticed how tall he was before, but that was probably why she was targeted. Virginia was tiny compared to most men. In fact, she was shorter than the majority of women. It had always been a point of contention for her.

"Do you want to go anywhere in particular?" Walt asked.

She stared at him and blinked. "I have no idea what is even here," she said. "Surprise me."

He looked thoughtful. "I'll show you where the stores are first. That way, you know where to go if you need any supplies."

Like clothes, she wanted to say, but refrained. She really did need to buy some gowns. The few clothes she had with her were not in good condition. Her wardrobe was meant to be replenished almost immediately after she arrived at her position, but things unfortunately changed rather quickly.

She forced a smile onto her face. "That sounds good. Sensible." He offered his arm for a second time, and Virginia hooked her arm through his.

They walked in silence for what seemed like forever, but it wasn't long before they arrived at the main street. "Promise me something," he said, his head turned to face her directly.

"I'll try."

"Do not walk down that laneway alone unless it's daylight. It's the only way back to the boarding house, but it's not safe at night." He pointed to where they'd just come from. "Mostly teenage boys hang out there, but we get a few unruly young men in town occasionally."

She swallowed. *Why was it that everywhere she went lately, danger abounded?* "I promise. I've had enough adventure to last a lifetime."

He nodded, and they continued. "This is the mercantile, and next door is the shoe shop. There's a diner over the road, the post office up the end there, and the butcher shop as well. You won't need food, as Miss Miller will keep your belly full." He grinned then. From what she'd seen so far, she also kept Walt's belly full. Perhaps not all the time, but at least some of the time.

Staring past the main street, she shivered. Virginia recognized the area she'd been lured to. It did not sit well with her, and the thought made her shudder. "What's wrong?" Walt's words surprised her. *Did he feel her tremble?* There could be no other explanation.

She pointed to the area she'd been taken. Virginia opened her mouth to speak, but no sound came out.

Walt wrapped an arm around her. "We won't be going there," he said firmly. "After what has occurred, I plan to have it blocked permanently. It is danger waiting to happen." He squeezed her hand and turned them both to face the other direction. "Let's go to the park. It's only small, but it's peaceful there." He didn't wait for an answer, and she didn't protest. She was enjoying his company, despite knowing she shouldn't.

Chapter Five

Walt reveled in the newcomer's company. He didn't know if it was the fragility she seemed to possess, or something entirely different.

What he did know was he felt good when he was around her. It was like a spark was set off in his heart. He'd lived in Shady Hollow for a few years now. Plenty of women had come and gone, but not one of them had affected him the way Virginia Black did.

In some ways, it frustrated him. The last thing Walt wanted was to be enamored with a complete stranger. Especially one who would leave town as quickly as she'd arrived. Truth be told, she would already have left if he hadn't said she needed to stay for the trial.

"It's so pretty here," Virginia said as she sat down at the park. "The flowers have a beautiful aroma." She leaned into them and breathed in. The smile on her face warmed him.

Walt had not originally intended to bring her here, especially with them being strangers. It was a little out of town, and away from most of the activity there. They were quite isolated, and given what

Virginia

she'd already endured today, now that he thought about it, coming here might not have been the best idea. "Without hiring a buggy, this is the prettiest place I could take you too."

She smiled again, and a shiver went down his spine. "Thank you. I really needed this after everything that's happened today." She frowned then. "What will happen? To that awful man, I mean?"

Virginia seemed more worried about the criminal than she did about her own welfare, and that bothered him. "He'll get jail time, but how much will be up to the judge. He didn't kill anyone, so he likely won't hang."

He watched as astonishment covered her face. "Hang?" Her hands went to her neck, and it was all he could do not to laugh.

"It could easily have been different. One victim was on death's door when she was discovered."

A small squeak left her mouth, and he wanted to put his arms around her and hold her close. She needed comfort, but it wasn't his place to do that. He barely knew the woman, and he was certain she would be furious if he tried.

Instead, he reached out and covered her hand. She glanced up at him, but didn't pull her hand away. His intention had been to comfort her, and yet, he felt soothed by the action.

"Miss Miller's boarding house is lovely. Thank you for arranging a room for me there." She seemed shy and glanced down into her lap as she spoke.

"My pleasure. Annie Miller will do anything for anyone. If you need something, ask. If she doesn't know the answer, she will surely find out."

She nodded then, as though she was unsure how to answer. "I guess we'd best get back. Can't be away too long. You never know when trouble will find its way into Shady Hollow." The moment the words were out, he wanted to take them back.

"Like the sort of trouble I brought." Her tone was self-loathing, but she had no need to feel guilty.

"That was not your fault. He did the same thing over and over, right here in town, but also in a variety of locations. We were bound to catch him." He faced her then. "I'm so glad we spotted him leaving the train station with you. Otherwise…" He swallowed down the emotion he suddenly felt. "who knows what might have happened."

All the color drained from her face. The last thing he wanted was to upset Virginia all over again. "Once the trial is over, you'll be able to put it all behind you." He stood then and held out a hand for her to stand. "We really should go. The last thing we want is for people to talk. There are plenty of gossips in town." He grimaced then. Walt knew only too well what gossip could do. He'd had to stop

Virginia

rumors far too many times, and even warn the gossip mongers to keep their opinions to themselves.

"I guess every town has them." She linked her arm through his, and they headed back to town, but not before he leaned down and broke off one of the brightest flowers that grew there and handed it to her. Virginia brought it to her face and breathed in its fragrance. "Thank you," she said.

Was it his imagination, or did he detect a skip in her steps?

Arriving back in town, he took Virginia to the mercantile, at her request. She wanted to purchase some clothes to see her through. "I'll wait for you," he said. "Make sure you get back safely." The look of horror on her face alerted him to the fact he'd scared her. "I promise there is nothing to be afraid of. John Doe is locked up and cannot lay a finger on you." The relief on her face was unmistakable.

He went outside and sat on the wooden bench. A couple of locals stopped to chat briefly, then went on their way. This was a lot of his job – talking to locals, getting information.

Walt glanced through the window of the mercantile and saw Virginia combing through the racks of gowns. There weren't a lot to choose from, being a rural town far from everywhere else, but they tried to keep a good range. The store was important to the town – he was the first to admit that. They were generous with their pricing, and didn't overcharge as far as he could tell. They easily could, being so isolated and away from the larger towns, but they did the right thing.

It wasn't long before the door rattled and the bell tinkled. He glanced up to see a beaming Virginia Black. "I bought some lovely garments," she said cheerfully. "These should get me through until the trial is over. I'm not sure what I'll do after that."

He didn't want to think what would happen after the trial. Virginia had already declared she would leave Shady Hollow, and for some bizarre reason, it left him feeling hollow. "I'm glad. Are you ready for me to walk you back to the boarding house, or do you have other shopping to do?"

She glanced down at the ground. "I'm keeping you from your work," she said as she bit her lower lip.

"This *is* my work. Protecting citizens is what I do." He offered his arm, and she took it. He also took her shopping bag. It wasn't heavy, but it was the right thing to do. He felt eerily comfortable with her by his side, and Walt wondered the reason behind it. *Was the fact he'd saved her cause some crazy protectiveness to kick in?* He honestly did not know.

Virginia

What he knew was he always felt good when she was around.

They walked silently down the laneway until they reached The Shady Hollow Boarding House for Women. He then escorted Virginia inside. The place was almost silent except for the sounds of Miss Miller moving about in the kitchen.

The woman was amazing. She ran the place basically alone. She had a lady come in to change the bedding every week, but apart from that, she was on her own. He'd been told she'd been doing that for several years, and he didn't doubt it. She ran it with such precision, like a well-oiled machine.

"It smells amazing in here," Virginia said.

He couldn't help but grin. "I told you Miss Miller is an excellent cook."

The person in question seemed to appear out of nowhere. "Ah, Miss Black, Marshal." She smiled then. "You are staying for supper, aren't you, Marshal?"

He blinked. There had been the occasional invitation to eat there, but not for some time. "Only if it's not too much trouble."

"For you, it is never any trouble," she said, her eyes darting from Walt to Virginia and back again. It was rather curious.

"That's settled then," she said, beaming. "Supper will be ready in one hour. You are welcome to stay until then, or return later. Your choice."

"Thank you. I have some paperwork to do, so I will come back."

He nodded to Virginia, then quickly left and headed to the Marshal's Office.

Walt flopped down onto the chair at his desk. "Problem?" Deputy Pete Ryan asked.

Walt frowned. "Nope." He flipped his feet up onto the desk and leaned back. "Annie Miller invited me to supper."

"And that's a problem how?" Pete studied him. "Oh, I know – it's that pretty little gal you rescued." He chuckled then.

"*We* rescued. I didn't do it alone. Besides, who said I was besotted with her?" Walt was getting annoyed with his deputy now.

This time, Pete laughed out loud. "You just did." He turned away then and went to his own desk.

Walt went over the conversation in his head and was startled when he recounted his words. *Since when did he use words like besotted?*

Virginia

Since Virginia Black arrived in town, that's when. He groaned out loud. "I have paperwork to do," he growled, and moved the papers on his desk from one spot to another. He continued to do that for the next half hour until he realized it was pointless. There was no hope of achieving anything the way he felt.

Instead, he went out the back to the jail where his prisoner was held. "What is your name?" he demanded, but got no response. "Doesn't matter to me, and won't matter to the judge," he told the prisoner. "You'll still be doing jail time for your crimes." He turned away then, but suddenly turned back. "What sort of coward preys on women? You'll go for attempted murder. Judge Cowley does not take to this sort of crime easily." He turned then, his anger boiling over. He knew if they didn't spot the man guiding Virginia, she might be…

He shook himself. The vision flashing through his mind was not a good one, and it left him not only furious, but feeling upset.

"He's not worth the time of day," Pete said. "His type never are." He left then, presumably to arrange a meal for their prisoner.

Walt found himself more annoyed over the fact he refused to give up his identity. His belongings revealed nothing, and he wasn't someone he'd come across before despite the man's repeated offenses.

Putting it all together now, Walt decided he'd ridden the trains, looking for victims. They'd discovered each of his victims had traveled by train the same day, which was how he and Pete came to be staking out the station. His heart had thudded when he'd seen the young woman being forced in the direction the prison wanted her to go, but at that point had no proof of his wrongdoings. He'd kept to the shadows and followed them. It could have been totally innocent, but he was almost positive the man's actions were far from it. And he was proven correct.

He pushed a few papers around again and discovered a large envelope under a pile of paperwork. It was not something he'd seen before and wasn't sure when it arrived. *It was quite possibly left there by the Postmaster this morning.* He quickly opened it, knowing what he would find inside. Wanted posters. *Could his man be amongst them?* Knowing his luck, it was highly unlikely.

He sorted through them, and luck was with him. The scratchy image of one Brutus Drake stared back at him. A smile played on his lips. Now he knew who the man was, he also knew what he'd done before the despicable deeds he'd performed in Shady Hollow. The man was even fool enough not to move outside their county. *Did he think the law here were idiots?* That riled Walt up even more.

For now, he would keep the knowledge between himself and his deputy. Pete would be as happy as he was, and would keep quiet. A weight seemed to be lifted from his shoulders.

The moment Pete returned, he would head off to Annie Miller's place. He was certain to enjoy the meal now. Not that there was ever any doubt.

Chapter Six

Two weeks had passed, and each time he saw Virginia, she seemed more nervous than the last. He was certain the judge would have arrived by now, but they simply had to wait it out. There was no other choice.

"Good evening, ladies," Walt said as he entered the boarding house dining room. He'd already removed his hat and coat, and left them at the entrance. He might be rough around the edges, but he was brought up to have manners. Especially when women were concerned.

He glanced across the table and found Virginia Black. A smile played on his lips. He knew he should refrain from any sign he was interested, especially before the trial, but he just couldn't help himself. "Miss Withers, Miss Carruthers, Miss Jacobson, Miss Black," he said as he nodded toward each woman. He'd already greeted Miss Miller when she let him in. Sensibly, she kept the front door locked at all times. You never knew who might wander in, and that would never do.

Until he'd arrived in town, the door was always open. After an incident with a drunk right there at the boarding house, he suggested keeping it locked.

Virginia

She'd done so ever since. Being at the end of a quiet lane, it wasn't located in easy view. Even if he was on Main Street itself, he couldn't see the building. He checked in there a few times a day when he was available, but that didn't mean the ladies were safe. Locking the door as a matter of habit eased his concern.

"You sit here, Marshal," Miss Miller said, indicating an empty seat next to Miss Black. The cheeky smile she threw him told Walt she was up to her old match-making tricks. If he wasn't in company, he would sigh deeply.

"Thank you, Ma'am," he said, and took his seat next to Virginia. She turned and smiled at him, and his heart fluttered.

"Hello again, Walt," she said, a coy smile on her face.

He felt heat travel up his face. What was it about this woman that had his heart racing? Well, he better stop having such thoughts about her – she was a victim, and he needed to treat her as such. He was certain the judge would not be happy if he found out.

Miss Miller went into the kitchen and returned with plates filled high. "Can I help with that?" Walt asked.

"You sit right where you are, and talk to the ladies," she answered, a grin on her face.

He knew where this was going, and he wasn't thrilled. He considered Annie Miller a friend, but pushing him toward Virginia Black was not playing fair. Especially given the situation. "Is that one of your new gowns?" he asked quietly.

"It is," she whispered. "Do you like it?"

It was beautiful and set his heart to racing even more. "I certainly do." He smiled then, and the smile she threw him sent a shiver down his spine. Virginia opened her mouth to speak, but a plate of food was put in front of them both.

"Link hands for the prayer of thanks, everyone." Miss Miller then said a few brief words, and they tucked in.

"This chicken pie is delicious, Miss Miller," Walt said after taking the first mouthful. "You are the best cook in town, by far." He then took another mouthful.

Mutterings of assent went around the table, and everyone continued to eat. When they finished, he sat back and rubbed his belly. "Best meal I've eaten since the last meal I had here." The ladies laughed at his words, but what he'd said was true.

Virginia

Pete was always jealous of his invitations, but knew his missus wouldn't be happy if he abandoned her cooking to come here.

"I hope you left room for dessert," his hostess said, a mock scowl on her face.

He chuckled then. "Since when did I miss out on dessert, Miss Miller?" The ladies joined in the laughter.

"Marshal, it is past time you called me Annie."

He nodded his assent.

Moments later, Virginia stood and collected the soiled dishes. No one asked her, she just did it. Walt was impressed by her actions. He pushed his chair back then, to help out as well. Annie flashed him a smile. "You sit down, Marshal. A hard-working man like you needs to be pampered now and then."

"But I…"

"But you nothing. Sit down," she said firmly. The other ladies chuckled. He sheepishly sat and didn't say another word until dessert was served. There was apple pie, along with cherry pie and clotted cream. "There's enough for everyone to have two slices of each. That means you too, Marshal," Annie said as she stared at him. He felt the heat rise in his face. He really needed to try to stop himself from feeling so embarrassed. A big man like him, doing a job like his, and he lets simple words turn his face red. Crazy.

Fresh coffee was poured into his mug after dessert was over, and they all retired to the sitting room. The chairs were big and comfortable, and he never refused the opportunity to sit in them. He sat down, and Virginia sat nearby. He told himself it was because he was the person she knew best. It wasn't untrue, but whether it was the true reason or not, he would not deny her company. In the short time she'd been here, he had become enamored with the young woman.

The sooner the trial was over and done with, the better. Then he could go back to his life of worrying about only himself. *The question was, would he then worry about where she was and what was happening to her?*

~*~

The postmaster hurried into the Marshal's Office. "I have a telegraph for you, Marshal. It's from the judge. He's arriving tonight."

Walt frowned. Since when did the postmaster think it was his duty to read the correspondence he received? "You are fully aware telegraphs are private. You're not meant to announce them."

"Sorry Marshal. I…" The look Walt gave him made the man hand over the telegraph and back out the

Virginia

door. He bumped into Pete as he left the office. "Sorry, Deputy," he said with a frown on his face.

"That's a lot of apologizing," Walt said under his breath.

Pete gazed at him. "What's going on?"

Walt waved the telegraph in the air. "Once again, my telegraph was read out loud by the postmaster." He grumbled then. It wasn't as big a deal as he made it out to be, but it certainly was annoying. "Anyway, Judge Cowley will be here tonight, so that means the trial will be tomorrow."

"You better get that girl of yours prepared. We both know it can be grueling."

Walt's head shot up. "She's not *my* girl. You are right though. She needs to be prepared." He stood then and headed toward the door. "I'd best go see her and explain what to expect. Same with Mabel Carruthers. She's agreed to testify as well."

Pete chuckled. "I'm surprised you even remembered Miss Carruthers exists," he joked. Walt was not impressed at his quip.

"For the last time, there is nothing going on between Virginia Black and me." He grabbed his hat and coat and stormed out of the room. He heard his deputy laughing as he left. The cheek of him. There was nothing between them, and there never would be.

Except he knew the last part might not be true. If he had his way, Walt would spend far more time with Miss Virginia Black. He would court her and see where it went. Trouble was, she planned to leave as soon as the trial was over and they locked Brutus Drake up. Hopefully, for a very long time.

He headed toward the boarding house with mixed feelings. He really needed to keep his distance, but he had no choice but to spend time with both ladies today and prepare them for tomorrow's proceedings.

Before he knocked on the boarding house door, he took some deep breaths.

Mabel Carruthers opened the door. "Marshal! What can I help you with? Did you want to see Miss Miller?" She stared at him curiously.

"I need to speak with both you and also Miss Black. I have news about the trial," Walt said.

"Oh," she said, and he watched the color drain from her face. "Come inside and sit down. I'll call Virginia for you. I mean Miss Black."

He watched as she went up the stairs. It wasn't long before the two ladies came into the sitting room. "You always look like you belong in that chair," Miss Carruthers told him, a smile on her face. "Would you like coffee, Marshal?"

"Of course he would," Annie Miller said, chuckling. "Our wonderful marshal never refuses coffee."

"This time I'm going to," he said firmly. "I need to speak to both ladies for a few minutes. Then I can take up your offer." He stood while the ladies each took a seat and waited for him to speak. "I've had word Judge Cowley will arrive tonight. The trial is set for tomorrow."

Virginia gasped. "I'm glad the day is finally coming, but I'm more nervous than ever now. It seems to have been such a long time since the…" She averted her eyes then.

"I've been here for well over a month," Miss Carruthers suddenly said. "I decided to stay permanently, since I love the town so much. Now my attacker is behind bars, I am going to see it through. I hope he gets life." She growled as she said the last sentence, and Walt felt for her. She had suffered a terrible attack, as well as losing a large sum of money.

"I've discovered a lot about the attacker, but I won't go into the details. You'll hear it all tomorrow, but I want you both to brace yourselves. The judge will ask you questions, and make his decision based on not only your testimony but also the man's past offences."

"I'm not sure I can do it," Virginia said, her voice low.

Mabel Carruthers reached out and squeezed her hand. "We'll do it together," she said, giving the other woman the reassurance she needed. He appreciated her words.

Walt explained a few details about the proceedings, and told them not to look at the prisoner, no matter what. "Well, that's it," Walt said, rubbing his hands together, knowing he was about to indulge in one of Annie Miller's feasts.

"Coffee is ready," his hostess called. Walt didn't hesitate to stand, following the ladies into the dining room.

Everyone was there, Virginia sitting in the same seat as last night, all designed by Miss Annie Miller, he was certain. Everyone was allocated a seat, and that's where they sat from then on. Not that he was complaining. He liked Virginia Black. Far too much, by his reckoning.

"What do you have planned for today, Marshal?" Annie sat a plate of oat cookies on the table, as well as a pound cake. She'd already distributed small plates to each person.

"Planning isn't something I get to do," he said grimly. "Things can change in a heartbeat." He glanced across at Virginia then, and she averted her

Virginia

eyes. Walt was certain she knew exactly what he meant. She'd found out the hard way how life could change without warning.

"Doc's the same. Things will be quiet, then suddenly everything changes." She sat down at the table then. "Well, come on, Marshal, ladies, tuck in."

He didn't wait to be told again. Walt reached for the pound cake – it was his favorite. Especially the way Annie made it. Sometimes she added orange juice to it for flavor, and it looked like she might even add some of the peel. He wasn't sure how she did that, but it sure tasted good.

When he glanced across at Virginia, she wasn't eating. She also wasn't drinking. "Don't worry about tomorrow," he whispered. "I'll be there to support you, along with Miss Carruthers." She nodded, but didn't appear assured. "It is an open and shut case. He's going away for a long time."

She shuddered. "I hope you're right. I… I don't feel safe, even knowing he's in jail. What if the judge lets him out?"

Walt's heart thudded. That couldn't happen. The man was also wanted in several other towns for various offences. *No judge would be that stupid. Would he?*

He shook himself mentally. Of course they wouldn't. Now he was thinking crazy-like. His heart was ruling his head, and he had to stop doing that. He knew from experience Judge Cowley was not a push-over. He didn't tolerate that sort of behavior.

Ever since Miss Virginia Black stepped foot in town, Walt hadn't been rational. That stopped now.

Virginia

Chapter Seven

Virginia dressed in one of her new gowns and pulled her hair into a neat style. She wore her best hat, and clutching her reticule, made her way down the stairs.

When she reached the last step, she took a fortifying breath, then let it out slowly. That was when she heard movement behind her. "Oh! Miss Carruthers," she said with a start. At least there would be two friendly faces there.

"Please, you must call me Mabel."

"And you should call me Virginia." She smiled then. Perhaps it was only brief, but she allowed herself to relax momentarily.

"If you're ready, we should go," Mabel said, and she hooked her arm through Virginia's. "The Marshal is meeting us there. He has to help the judge prepare for the trial."

Virginia felt the shudder that traveled from her head to her toes and wanted nothing more than to turn around and hide away in her cozy room. Her room had become her refuge. After today, once the trial was over, she did not know what she would do.

The last thing on her mind was returning to her father's home. That would never happen. Not while she had funds to support herself, anyway. With her money locked away in a safe at the Marshal's Office, at least she knew it was secure. If it wasn't for her new friend, Marshal Walt Riley, she would have nothing. Not a cent to her name, and possibly not even her life. "I… I don't think I can face him," she told Mabel, her voice barely visible.

Mabel's hand clasped hers. "Yes, you can. We will do it together," she said firmly, then led them out the door and onto the street. "See that building? The one with the fancy woodwork outside? That's the courthouse." She turned to Virginia and studied her. "We are going to walk there together and tell our stories. We are going to tell the judge everything that happened, and see that horrible, horrible man put away for a very long time."

"I," Virginia swallowed back her fear. "Of course we are. They can't let him out again."

Mabel studied Virginia, her face solemn. "He *will* go to jail. Our testimonies will help the judge decide exactly how long he'll be there. Come on," she said then, putting a cheerful smile on her face. "We can't keep the judge waiting."

Virginia and Mabel sat on the front bench where Walt Riley had placed them. Judge Cowley sat

Virginia

ominously at the front, reading through the paperwork the marshal had provided him with. Every now and then the judge grunted and glanced toward the prisoner who was handcuffed and sat away from the witnesses. He scowled at the prisoner more than once. Marshal Riley sat in the front with the two witnesses.

"That's a good sign," Walt whispered to the women, then studied the judge again.

Judge Cowley turned to face the prisoner. "Brutus Drake, you are charged with multiple counts of robbery, attempted robbery, assault, attempted murder and whatever else I can drag up to charge you with." He glared at the prisoner, who seemed shocked the judge knew his name. "How do you plead?"

"Not guilty."

An audible gasp filled the courthouse. Walt chuckled quietly. Virginia figured it was at the man's audacity.

Walt was called up to testify, and read out the victim's statements, then took his seat again.

"I'd like to hear from the witnesses now," Judge Cowley demanded. Virginia did not want to cross that man – he appeared to be quite ferocious. He glanced down at his paperwork. "Miss Black, you're up first. Sit here," he said, indicating a nearby chair.

She stood, despite her legs feeling like jelly. Virginia was convinced she would collapse on the floor at any moment. She glanced at Mabel, who sent her a reassuring smile, then Walt, who did the same.

She kept her head high, and didn't look toward the prisoner, as Walt had suggested. *Watch me, or the judge,* he'd instructed. *The prisoner is insignificant.* She took a deep breath and tried to stop the trembling that had overtaken her body.

"Tell us what happened," Judge Cowley said in a fatherly manner, making her feel more at ease.

She turned to face the judge and caught a glimpse of the prisoner. "I met him on the train, and he seemed nice," she said, as her heart pounded in her head. "He asked me to coffee, and I accepted, but then…" She stopped talking, uncertain she could replay the trauma of what happened that day.

"You are safe here, Miss Black. No one can harm you. Please continue."

Virginia then relayed how he'd tricked her and forced her into that dreadful area where he tried to rob her. It took all her resolve not to break down.

"Thank you, Miss Black. Is there anything else you'd like to add?" The judge nodded as though encouraging her.

"I don't feel safe now," she said, her voice barely audible. "I'm afraid to go out alone now." She said, this time her voice was far louder. It was as though she wanted the Brutus Drake to know what he'd done to her, although she was certain he didn't care.

"Thank you, Miss Black. You may return to your seat." Virginia did as she was told, and a wave of relief passed through her.

"Miss Mabel Carruthers. Please take the stand." Virginia reached for her friend's hand and squeezed it. Mabel had been waiting for this moment far longer than Virginia had. "Please tell us what occurred."

Mabel glanced across at the prisoner and glared at him, then a tiny smile played on her lips as if she was sending him a message. One that said *you're going away for a very long time.* "I also met the accused on the train. He helped me after the train jolted me to the floor." Virginia gasped. That was the exact same scenario she had encountered. "Then he offered to take me for coffee. Such a delightful fellow he was too, until he lured me to a quiet laneway and tried to rob me. When I fought back, he tried to bash my head in." She pulled her hair back. "You can still see the scars, Judge Cowley."

The judge's expression was now one of fury. "Is there anything else you would like to say, Miss Carruthers?"

She glanced first at the judge, then at her attacker. "Yes, I would. I hope you rot in jail for the rest of your life, you lowlife mong…"

"Thank you, Miss Carruthers," Judge Cowley said, barely containing his laughter. "You may return to your seat. The last witness is Doctor Sherman Henderson. Please take the stand, Doctor."

Virginia turned as the doctor was called. She hadn't known he was here. As she glanced around the courtroom, she spotted Annie Miller sitting in the public gallery.

"I believe you were the one to patch up Miss Carruthers, Doctor Henderson?"

"That is correct, Judge. She was in a terrible state when Marshal Riley found her, and to be honest, I wasn't certain she would live. Miss Carruthers needed ten stitches to her head and neck, and another five on her arm. She'd also lost a lot of blood." He glared at the man on the stand. "If I may, Judge, Miss Black was also in need of medical attention. The Marshal and Deputy saved her from injury, but she still needed my help."

"Thank you, Doctor Henderson. You may step down now."

Virginia

The doctor took his place at the back of the courtroom again. Annie Miller slipped her hand into the doctor's hand, and Virginia was taken aback.

The courtroom was quiet, and all eyes were trained on Judge Cowley as he wrote notes on the papers he had in front of him. "I'm ready to make my judgement," he said, glancing around the room. He nodded at Walt. Virginia wasn't sure what that was about. "I find the prisoner guilty of all charges. Since his actions have put the lives of many women at risk, and left several on the brink of death, I hereby sentence him to…" There was a scuffle at the back of the room and the judge looked up to see what was going on.

"Deputy, arrest that man!"

Deputy Pete Nolan grabbed the man who had caused the interruption, but missed. Virginia gasped when she saw the gun in his hand. "He has a gun!" she shouted, and Walt jumped up from his seat at the front of the room.

"Get down!" he shouted to the women, pushing them both to the floor. Her heart pounded, and terror ran through her. *What would happen now?* Her biggest concern was for the marshal and his deputy.

She glanced across the room at Brutus Drake and noticed he was grinning. *Was this an attempt to break him out of jail?*

Virginia was light-headed, and her heart continued to pound. She couldn't believe what was going on around her.

Suddenly the second man ran past them, toward the prisoner, Walt grabbed him. The deputy was only a few steps behind. They both jumped at the intruder, but not before he got off a round, hitting Brutus Drake in the shoulder. Brutus screamed out in pain. Virginia knew it was horrible of her, but she didn't care. The man was revolting. He didn't care about anyone else.

Walt and Pete wrestled the other man to the ground and handcuffed him. Judge Cowley stood to the side of the room and out of the way of harm during the tussle. The two women held each other as they cowered under the wooden bench.

When everything was calm again, Doc Henderson went to the prisoner. "It's just grazed," he said. "It's barely worth mentioning." Brutus bared his teeth, but no one cared.

Walt helped the ladies to their feet. They brushed themselves off and took their seats once again.

After being appropriately restrained, the intruder, Crandall Orwell, was charged and tried right there and then. He was sentenced to three years' in jail. "Now I shall finish what I started earlier," Judge Cowley said. "Brutus Drake, you are a danger to society. I believe even as an old man, you will be

Virginia

dangerous. I therefore sentence you to life in prison, never to be released." He then slammed down his gavel and stood. "Thank you, everyone, especially to our very brave witnesses. Without you, we would not have the same outcome."

"I'll stop by later," Walt told the women quietly. "We have to get these two behind bars."

Both Pete and Walt grabbed the prisoners and lead them to the jail. "I'm bleeding," Brutus complained. "I have a right to be seen by a doctor."

"You've seen the doctor, and he said you're fine." Walt glared at both men.

Brutus turned to his friend. "This is your fault. You always were a hapless fool." He shoved his so-called friend away with his shoulder. If it hadn't been so serious, it would have been laughable.

"We could put them in the same jail cell and let them kill each other," Walt said, half joking. "It would save the county a lot of money."

"Good idea," the judge said. "It would rid us of the scum." He grinned then, and walked out of the room, taking all his paperwork with him. Luckily, Virginia knew they were joking.

Once the prisoners were both removed from the courtroom, Virginia and Mabel returned to the boarding house. Annie Miller wasn't far behind, along with the doc. *Was she to believe the two were seeing each other?*

"We all need a good, strong cup of coffee," Annie said as she unlocked the boarding house door. "Doc is joining us, too. I wonder how long the marshal will be." She shrugged her shoulders then.

"You never can tell," Doc said. "Anything can happen at the drop of a hat. I didn't expect the drama we had in the courtroom today. It all seemed quite black and white." He frowned then. "I guess it was, but the second man arriving made for a more thrilling procedure."

Annie swiped at his arm. "It was far from thrilling – it was downright terrifying. And these two very brave ladies were right in the middle of it," she said, admonishing the doctor. Then she leaned into him and the doc put his arms around her.

Suddenly their hostess pulled back. "Sit down, ladies. I'm sure you need time for your hearts to calm down to a normal pace."

Mabel and Virginia turned to each other. They both agreed it was far too much excitement for one day. They sat at the table, and coffee was placed in front of them. It wasn't long before there was a knock at the door.

Marshal Walt Riley was greeted, and looked like he really needed that coffee.

Virginia

Chapter Eight

"I guess you're both leaving town soon," Walt said as he sipped his coffee. "Now the court case is over." His heart was breaking. Both women had become friends, but Virginia had become much more than that to him. Not that she knew. Nor did she reciprocate his feelings.

Mabel was the first to speak. "I'm contemplating staying. I've come to like this little town. And I do love living here at the boarding house. Annie has made me feel very welcome."

Their hostess smiled.

He turned to Virginia then. "What about you? Are you staying or leaving?"

She shrugged her shoulders. "I don't know what I'm doing. I'll have to think about it. Right now, I have nowhere else to go."

"You must have a home to go to," he said carefully. He had no idea of her situation. "Parents?"

She closed her eyes momentarily, and he watched as she breathed deeply and let it out slowly. It seemed to be a habit she had when pondering how to answer. "My mother is long gone, my father is oppressive. He tried to force me into an unwanted marriage. It's the reason I left to begin with."

"I'm sorry," Walt said. *What else was there to say?*

"I'll stay here for another day or two at least, before deciding."

He nodded. There was no hiding the fact he was disappointed. He'd come to think of Virginia Black fondly. Given the chance, he felt sure she would like him. So far, the opportunity hadn't arisen. He wanted to blurt out all his feelings, but knew that wasn't a good idea. At least not in company.

He gulped back his coffee. His disappointment threatened to overtake him. Walt needed to get out of there before he allowed his feelings to show. It was the last thing he wanted to happen. Virginia did not need anyone making her feel she needed to stay, especially not him.

Walt emptied his mug and pushed back his chair.

"Leaving already?" Annie Miller seemed surprised. "I thought you might take Miss Black for a stroll. She's had a difficult day." She glanced across the table then. "Of course, so has Miss Carruthers."

Mabel's head shot up. "I'm fine, thank you. I…" She studied Virginia briefly. "I need to lie down for a nap." She feigned tiredness, but Walt saw right through her.

Virginia

He wanted to spend time with Virginia, but the fact she would leave Shady Hollow soon meant it was in his best interest to break all ties. Otherwise, his heart would be ripped to shreds. It was already damaged, and he didn't need more grief.

He'd been put on the spot, and had little choice other than to ask her to accompany him. "That would be rather pleasant," he said instead. "Would you join me, Miss Black?" he asked, trying to mask his heartache.

A smile played on her face, but Walt felt certain she felt the same way he did. *Since they would part ways in a matter of days, what was the point of getting to know each other better?*

Virginia stood then. "I think I would enjoy that. The proceedings were rather… traumatic." She glanced down at her entwined hands. "To be honest, I'm glad that is now behind us."

They walked to the front door together, then she headed upstairs for her coat. The days were getting colder, and they needed to be prepared. He reached for his own coat and waited for Virginia to return. On hearing her door clicking closed, his head shot up, and he stared as she came down the stairs. His heart fluttered, simply watching her. Walt had never felt this way before.

As she reached the bottom of the stairs, he reached out a hand to her. "You look beautiful," he said. Color flooded her cheeks, and she averted her eyes. "Thank you," she near whispered. "I've only added my coat, nothing more." A smile played on her lips then, and joy spread through him. *What would he do when she was gone?*

The thought entered his mind that he needed to find a way to keep her here.

~*~

"I didn't realize Shady Hollow was quite so big," Virginia said.

Walt stared at her. "Big? Shady Hollow?" He grinned then. "Not really."

Her heart fluttered. "I guess not, but it's bigger than I initially thought. My first impression was a tiny town with less than a handful of stores."

"It's not quite that small, but we get by. I've been assigned to several towns over the years. This is my favorite by far. I hope I get to stay here for a very long time." He glanced about. "This business with Brutus Drake is the only true criminal activity I've encountered here. We have our drunks and pilfering, but nothing major until recently." He studied her, and it unnerved Virginia. "It's a truly wonderful place to live."

Virginia

Why did she get the feeling his statement was directed at her, and only her? She'd only been here for a few weeks, but whenever she saw Walt, she got the feeling he was interested in her as more than just a witness. She swallowed before answering. "It seems a nice place to live. Annie Miller is lovely, along with the ladies living there."

"Of course, it's nothing like Billings," he said, referencing her home town. "We don't have the enormous stores you have there. Nor do we have the nightlife – parties, theater, balls, and all that sort of thing."

Virginia wondered if he was trying to talk her into staying, but suddenly he went the other way. Perhaps he wanted her to leave after all. "I have never attended a ball, or a party," she said. "I'm not interested in such things. I prefer the quiet life."

He smiled and guided her toward one of the wooden benches outside the courthouse. "Do you want to go home, or continue our stroll?" She had never really taken a lot of notice before. He was the marshal after all, and had been working with her to jail a criminal. But now things had shifted, they were becoming friends. Seeing him for the first time as a man, Walt Riley was a very handsome man. He was tall, good looking, and his blue eyes were quite striking. Virginia stared at his face and couldn't pull her gaze away.

She'd come to enjoy their strolls each day. Just having him near had become the highlight of her day; she didn't want to think about them not continuing.

"Was that a no?"

What did she miss? He'd clearly said something, but she was woolgathering and totally missed what he'd said. "Sorry, I was far away." She felt the heat rise from her neck and into her cheeks. He laughed, and the sound lifted her spirits. "What was the question?"

"I asked if you would like to go for a drive into the hills. I could hire a buggy from the livery, and…"

"Yes!" She was a little too enthusiastic, Virginia was certain. She really wanted to see more of this town. It definitely wasn't about spending time with Walt — that would be a silly assumption. They barely knew each other.

He grinned down at her. "We could have a picnic. That would allow us a little longer time. I'm sure Annie would be fine with that."

"I'll have to let her know."

Walt nodded, and they headed back to the boarding house.

Virginia

"You arrange the buggy, Marshal, and I'll pack a picnic basket for you." Annie seemed far more pleased than Virginia had expected.

"There's no need to do that. I can get something from the bakery," Walt told her. "I certainly don't expect you to supply our lunch."

"Don't argue. It will take but a minute of my time." She waved him away. "You go to the livery while I do this."

Walt turned on his heel and left the boarding house, saying he would return shortly. It was now clear to Virginia – Walt and her were being pushed together. It was the last thing she wanted. He was a nice man, and good looking, but she wasn't interested in being paired, and she certainly wasn't interested in getting married. Especially to someone who lived such a dangerous life.

When she was ready to marry, she wanted the person to live a far more sedate life. A mercantile owner, or someone who ran a café, would be a far better choice. She sighed. Why did everyone try to marry her off? Just because she was of an age to marry didn't mean she had to marry. It wasn't as though she was in love. Especially not with Walt. He was a friend, and nothing more. The fact her stomach fluttered whenever he was near meant absolutely nothing.

Annie sent her upstairs to tidy up. Not that she needed to do that. She was quite presentable as she was, but Virginia did as she was told. She hurried up the stairs and, staring into the mirror, saw she really did need to straighten up. Her hair was unraveling. It had been a little windy today, and that was the only explanation she could come up with.

She pulled the pins out of her hair and brushed it vigorously. Once she was satisfied, she styled it once again. She turned her head this way and that, ensuring she was satisfied with the result. Then she pulled her bonnet on, making sure she had no stray pieces of hair hanging down.

It wasn't long before there was a knock on the front door. She knew it would be Walt, and her heart fluttered. The fact surprised her. She wasn't interested in the handsome marshal. In fact, she wasn't interested in anyone. But she would like to see more of Shady Hollow before she decided about relocating here, or leaving in the next day or so.

She hurried down the stairs. It was a dangerous move, because she tripped when she was almost at the bottom. Virginia tried to save herself, but it was too late. She fell forward and disaster loomed.

Until she felt herself being gripped. Two powerful hands held her and pulled her close. "Steady on." Walt's gentle voice startled her. She had been in such a hurry she hadn't even noticed him there. He

Virginia

lifted her from the steps and placed her on the ground, holding on to her, ensuring she was steady before he let go.

She glanced up at him, then averted her eyes. "Thank you. I feel so embarrassed."

"No need to feel that way. I have the buggy," he said, changing the subject completely.

"And your picnic is ready," Annie said as she entered the foyer. "Have a lovely time, you two," she said, as she winked at Walt. "Oh, and there's a blanket in the picnic basket." She turned and left them without another word.

"Do you get the feeling…"

"I do," Walt said. "That's Annie Miller for you. She's long been a match-maker around here. We can ignore that and just enjoy the day."

Her heart thudded. He had made it perfectly clear he wasn't interested in her at all. Walt only wanted to show her around, nothing more. Virginia planted a smile on her face and walked ahead of him when he waved her ahead.

Her mind was made up. She would work out exactly where she wanted to go, and would leave Shady Hollow within the week.

"It's a pleasant drive," Walt said as he held the reins. "It's been some time since I came up here, but I still remember the best places. There's a small stream close to here," he said, pointing to his left. "It's a delightful spot for a picnic."

She glanced about – it was a magnificent area. If Walt hadn't brought her up there, Virginia wouldn't have known just how beautiful it was. The air was chilly, but her warm coat helped with that.

"There are some lovely places to go for a walk, too. It's not so dense we would get ourselves lost." Her head shot up then. *Should she be worried?* "I promise you're safe with me," he said, half laughing. "I want to go back to my warm bed tonight. It gets quite cold up here at night this time of year."

"You know this how?" she asked in disbelief.

Walt stared at her momentarily. "A young boy was lost here a while back. We had a search party out to look for him. We stayed out all night."

Virginia could have kicked herself. Of course he would do that. Walt wasn't the sort to leave a child alone up here at night without doing everything possible to locate him. "Did you find him?" She braced herself for the worst.

"We did. Apart from shivering from the cold, he was in a pretty good condition."

Virginia

Virginia did not know why, but she sighed with relief. He was staring at her in confusion. "Lucky for the boy, he'd been taught survival skills from a young age. Otherwise, who knows what the outcome might have been?" He pulled into a clearing and brought the horse to a stop. Walt pulled on the brake and jumped down, then hurried around to help her down. Not that Virginia needed helping — she was quite independent. She'd needed to be to survive.

He reached up and held her around the waist. A tingle went through her, and she glanced down into his face. Walt stared at her and slowly lifted her to the ground. In a split second, his expression changed. His face softened, and he looked at her in the strangest way.

Ever so gently, he placed her on the ground, his hands never leaving her. He continued to hold her around the waist, then leaned in toward her. The movement was so slow as to be almost unseen, but bit by bit, he got closer. Virginia swallowed, then licked her lips.

Was he going to kiss her? She was convinced he was. *She was confused then – should she let him kiss her? Or would it change everything between them?*

The more she thought about it, the more she believed this would be the case. They would no longer be friends, and then she would be in a real conundrum. A new decision would have to be made. If Walt kissed her, Virginia would have to confess she'd been compromised. No decent man would be interested in someone whose reputation had been sullied in that way.

She stared into his beautiful blue eyes. She couldn't pull her gaze away from them, and it was her undoing. Those few seconds she'd been mesmerized, his lips connected with hers.

They were soft and gentle. He didn't force his lips on hers, merely brushed them across hers. She should push him aside, stop him from taking liberties with her. Virginia didn't want to do that. It felt good with him so close. He tasted good.

She closed her eyes, and a shudder went through her. His hands came up and cupped her face. His hands were soft, gentle, and she felt like she would melt. Then suddenly they were gone. His closeness was gone.

Her eyes fluttered open.

He stood staring down at her, his expression one of disgust.

Virginia

Chapter Nine

Walt stepped back abruptly.

He had no right to treat her like this. To kiss Virginia with no expectation of it happening. He'd not told her how he felt, and she'd not expressed any interest in him. He was utterly disappointed with himself. And truth be told, disgusted.

No decent man treated women this way. He should have asked her first. *If he had, would she have agreed?* Probably not. He had given her the choice, but in his mind, that's what he'd done by moving in slowly. In reality, he decided, that wasn't what he'd done at all. "I'm sorry," he grumbled. His words changed her expression to disappointment.

"For what? Kissing me?" She smiled then, as though she'd enjoyed it. He couldn't see how that would be the case at all.

"I had no right…"

"I liked it," she whispered. "I wasn't expecting it, but it was nice." She had a dreamy expression on her face, and it made his heart flutter. Where they went from there, he did not know. Virginia made no commitment about her feelings for him, but neither had he.

"We should set up for the picnic," he said, changing the subject completely. It was becoming awkward between them, and it was the last thing he wanted to happen.

He flicked the blanket out over the grass and placed the basket in the middle. Virginia sat down in that elegant way she had of doing things, and he just dropped down. They were on opposite sides of the blanket, which suited him fine. This way, he couldn't let his heart rule his common sense. If they'd sat closer, it might tempt him to kiss her again.

Virginia looked inside the basket and pulled the items out, one by one. "It all looks delicious," she said, glancing up at him. "Sandwiches and cake. There's even some water." She pushed some sandwiches toward him, and Walt reached out to take them. Their hands touched, and a tremor raced up his arm.

This was a bad idea. One of the worst he'd ever had. In a few days, they would bid each other farewell forever, and he would likely wave her goodbye at the train station. His only hope was she had nowhere to go. Never would he have thought that a good thing. She wasn't exactly homeless, but deciding not to return to her father's home meant she didn't have a place to go.

Virginia

With the money her former employer had given her, Virginia had enough to set up a small home here in Shady Hollow. *The question was, would she?*

"It's so peaceful here," she said, bringing him back to the present. "I can't recall ever being somewhere so beautiful."

He unwrapped his lunch and took a bite, glancing about. He'd been here several times before but hadn't appreciated it the way Virginia did. But she was right. It was peaceful. The trees and shrubs made it look quite beautiful. "You're right," he said. "I've never really appreciated its beauty before." He took another bite. Anything to avoid talking about *that moment* they'd shared earlier. "About before…"

She cut him off. "It was as much my fault as yours. I didn't stop you." On reflection, she was right. He'd kissed her, but she didn't tell him no, and she hadn't pushed him away. Even so, he instigated it.

Virginia smiled at him, but Walt wasn't convinced her smile was genuine. She could easily be covering her disgust for him. They were alone up here in the hills, and she had no way to get back to town without him. She could merely be humoring him.

He finished eating his sandwiches, and Virginia pushed a plate of cake toward him, then poured them each a mug of water. Annie Miller had thought of everything. His disgust for himself made it hard to swallow even the delicious cake in front of him.

"Would you like to go for a stroll? I promise to keep my hands to myself." His tone should tell her how much he admonished himself for his earlier actions.

"I *would* like to go for a stroll." She packed the basket up, and he placed it, along with the blanket, on the buggy. "We won't get lost, will we?" she asked, feigning concern. It made him chuckle and lightened his mood.

"I promise we won't get lost. I will keep you safe from any wild creatures, too," he said. *But who would keep her safe from him?* Walt was far too smitten with his witness and wasn't sure he could keep his distance. He wanted to kiss her again and again, but knew that would push the boundaries.

"Wild creatures?" She appeared horrified until he laughed. She punched his arm then, realizing he was joking with her. She stared up into his face, then stepped forward. His heart pounded. Her expression was one of want. At the same time, she looked confused. Her arms went up around his neck and she pulled him down to her.

"You don't have to do this," he whispered.

"I want to," she whispered back. "Are you denying me?"

Virginia

He grinned then. "Never." Their lips met, only this time, she was the one who initiated the kiss. His arms went around her back and he pulled her closer still. He breathed in her perfume, and he wanted nothing more than to tug the pins from her hair and let it fall free.

Walt knew if he did that, tongues would wag when they got back, and it was the last thing he wanted to happen. For her sake.

He relished the feel of her skin on his. Savored her nearness. If he could stay like this forever, he would be in his element. "I've become very fond of you," he whispered against her ear. "More than fond. I'm falling in love with you." She stilled, and it bothered him. *Had Walt unintentionally scared her away?* It was the last thing he intended to do. "Virginia?"

She pushed herself away from him. Her face was ashen, and he wasn't sure if that meant she didn't reciprocate his feelings, or it was another reason entirely. She glanced up at him, her eyes wary. "That's not a good idea," she said, then turned away from him.

Her behavior confused him. One minute she was instigating a kiss, and next... *What on earth was going on?* He gently turned her to face him again. Before he had an opportunity to question her, Virginia spoke.

"You don't want to get mixed up with the likes of me. I should never have agreed to come with you today." Sadness shadowed her face, and tears danced on her lashes. "Just being with me could ruin your reputation." Her words were full of emotion, and it broke his heart. The moment the words were out, tears flooded her cheeks.

"Wha…?" He shook his head. The day had begun as a happy one, but something had changed all that. It was him. He'd ruined everything by kissing her, then declaring his love for her. He was such a fool.

She brushed at her tears, but they were relentless and continued to fall. "It's not your fault. It's mine." He stepped forward and brushed her hot tears away. She closed her eyes and leaned her face into his hand. That simple action told Walt she had feelings for him, but for whatever reason, she was afraid to let her feelings show. "You don't want someone like me. There are other women who would make you happy." She glanced up at him and he recognized the torture on her face. "Mabel would be a good choice." A small sob escaped her as she voiced the words.

Mabel? He wasn't interested in Mabel Carruthers, and she had no interest in him. The only person he had feelings for was the one standing in front of him now. He reached out and pulled her close to his chest. His hand cupped her head and held her close.

This woman, who he believed was his soulmate, was torturing herself, but he had no inkling why.

"Tell me what happened," he whispered. His heart was shattering, not knowing what was wrong or how he could fix it.

She glanced up at him, her eyes red and puffy. "I…" She swallowed back the emotion he saw teetering on the edge once more. "I was put in a compromising position." She turned her head away then, but he was certain it wasn't before she noticed the shocked expression on his face.

"Compromised?" he asked, trying to pull himself together. "In what way?" No matter what she told him, Walt wanted to marry her. He was drawn to her, and had been from that very first moment they met. She seemed somehow vulnerable, and not just because of the robbery. There was something else – he hadn't been able to put his finger on it before, now it was all becoming clear.

"It was because of my new position as governess," she began, and told him the entire story. By the time she finished, his coat was near drenched. But Walt didn't care. He didn't care about her supposedly ruined reputation, either. Nothing had happened, and even if it had, he would be there to support her. He loved the woman he held in his arms.

He leaned in and kissed her forehead. "I don't care about any of that," he whispered. "I only care that you were not harmed by any of it." She sobbed again, and he pulled her even tighter to him. "I want to marry you." He sighed then. "But I suppose I have to court you first. Propriety expects it."

His heart thudded as he waited for her reply. *Why would she want to marry a man like him? A marshal who was always in danger and never knew what would happen from one day to the next?*

"Yes," she whispered.

He shook his head in confusion. "Yes, what?"

Virginia laughed. "Yes, I'll marry you. I don't care about courting. I am already far too fond of you. The barrier that kept me from you is no longer there. Provided you're certain it's what you want."

He reached down and lifted her from the ground. "I'm certain," he said, swinging her around in his arms. "We'll have to talk to the preacher when we get back."

"Not today," Virginia said firmly. "I must look a fright."

"You are beautiful," Walt said. "The most beautiful woman I've ever known." He kissed her then and put her gently to the ground.

Walt stared at her. He couldn't comprehend the fact she'd agreed to marry him. Him! *Why would anyone want to marry him?* He would be eternally grateful

Virginia

to Virginia for accepting his proposal. The next thing he needed to do, after talking to the preacher, was buy a wedding ring.

"Are we going for that stroll, or must we go home?" She averted her face, and he was certain she didn't want him to see her face. Her eyes were red and puffy, but it didn't make her any less appealing to him.

He moved in front of her, ensuring he could see her face completely. "If you're really worried about your appearance, I'll take you down to the stream." He'd heard women talk about this old trick – splashing cold water on their eyes was meant to hide the redness.

A small smile played on her lips. "I would appreciate it," she said quietly. "I don't want people knowing how upset I've been. Or why."

Walt wrapped an arm around her, and warmth filled him. He had been blessed the day he met Virginia Black, even if it was under horrific circumstances.

Chapter Ten

The drive home was mostly in silence. According to Walt, the cold water of the stream had done the trick and her eyes were no longer red. She had no way of knowing if that was true, but had to trust what he told her.

He still wanted to visit the preacher today, but her head was spinning, and Virginia wanted to put it off. As a compromise, Walt would collect her in the morning, and they would visit the preacher together.

It all seemed so sudden. She wasn't having second thoughts, but she wondered what the townsfolk would say about Virginia snapping up their handsome marshal. Especially the single women who, according to Walt, had tried desperately to get him to marry them.

Would that cause bad feelings between those women and Virginia? She certainly hoped not. Destiny brought her to Walt. Some might call it fate. Either way, she knew now they were meant to be.

Annie Miller answered the door when Walt knocked. She appeared rather sheepish, and Virginia wondered what had caused her reaction. "Coffee is ready," she said, diverting attention when Virginia studied her. As they moved into the

Virginia

kitchen, she noticed Doc Henderson sitting at the table.

He looked sheepish as well. *What had they missed?*

"We have an announcement," Walt said.

Virginia sighed. She'd hoped to keep their decision to themselves for another day, at least. Until they'd spoken to the preacher. Right now, it didn't feel final. Perhaps after speaking with him tomorrow, things would be different.

Annie rubbed her hands together with glee. "I hope it's what I think it will be." Her smile was so wide, Virginia couldn't help but smile as well.

Walt reached for her hand and pulled Virginia close. "I proposed and Virginia accepted. We're going to see the preacher tomorrow."

Annie moved so quickly, Virginia was startled when the older woman moved in and hugged her. Then she moved onto Walt. "I'm so happy for you both," she said, still beaming.

"Congratulations," Doc Henderson echoed. "I can't say I'm surprised." He reached out then and took Annie's hand.

There had been brief hints the two were seeing each other. They'd sat together at the courthouse, and she'd noticed their intertwined hands now and then.

And the doc had coffee and meals there often. Just as Walt did.

How could she have been so blind to their situation? She shook her head. "Congratulations to you as well?" she asked warily.

The two glanced at each other then. "We spoke to the preacher today. He can marry us the day after tomorrow." Doc Henderson grinned then. "We've kept it quiet for a very long time. Now the time is right."

Annie glanced from the doc to Virginia and Walt. "How do you feel about a double wedding?" Her cheeks turned a bright red. Suddenly, her eyes opened wide. "Forget I said that. It would be an imposition, I'm sure."

Virginia clapped her hands together. "How wonderful would that be? What do you think, Walt?"

"I think," he said, wrapping his arms around her, "it would be amazing. I can't think of anything better than sharing our wedding with our two best friends." He kissed Virginia's forehead then, and she leaned into him.

Her heart fluttered at the thought in only two more days she would be Mrs. Walt Riley.

~*~

Virginia

The day of the wedding seemed to come around slowly. Virginia awoke early. *How could she sleep with such a momentous day looming?*

The two women had visited *Boutique Gowns* and had each chosen a dress. Mabel Carruthers and Caroline Jacobson had offered to fix their hair, and Ginny Withers, the other boarder, arranged their flowers and made sure everything went to plan.

She also ensured the two grooms did not enter the building until after the wedding.

The two brides hugged each other. Virginia felt as though she was in a daze. Less than a month ago, she was at her father's house, fighting off totally unsuitable admirers.

Today she was preparing to walk down the aisle with the man of her dreams. She glanced at herself in the mirror. "You should set up a hairdressing shop," she said, and meant it. "Perhaps you and Caroline could go into business together."

The two temporary hairdressers smiled at each other. "What a great idea!" Mabel said, sounding even more excited than she'd been all morning.

Annie glanced at Virginia, taking a huge breath, then letting it out. "Are you ready?"

"I… I think so," Virginia said. "What about you?"

"I have waited for this day for years. Watching you and Walt spurred Sherman on." She smiled then. "I can't thank either of you enough." She hugged Virginia again.

"Be careful of your hair," Mabel said a little louder than she normally spoke. "Ladies, beautiful brides," she said as she beamed, "it is time to leave." She herded the two women down the stairs and through the front door, where two buggies stood, waiting to ferry them to the church.

The church wasn't far from the boarding house, but their grooms were considerate of the brides and their beautiful gowns. It wasn't snowing but was a little chilly. Both brides placed their coats on their shoulders for extra warmth and were soon on their way to get married.

Their friends held the church doors open when they arrived. Organ music was playing, and it soothed Virginia's nerves somewhat. Annie reached for her hand and squeezed it. Deputy Pete Nolan stood at the back of the church, waiting for them. He would lead the brides down the aisle, one on each arm.

The three boarders hurried to the front of the church and sat down. Electricity filled the air. There were far more people in the little church than Virginia expected. Word had obviously spread around Shady Hollow that three of the town's prominent citizens

Virginia

were marrying today. Everyone evidently wanted to be a part of it.

As she walked past, Mabel clutched at Virginia's hand. *Was that tears she saw in the other woman's eyes?* Oh dear. She hoped Mabel didn't set her off. She'd shed more than enough tears recently to last her a lifetime.

As the brides reached the front, their grooms reached out and took their respective bride's hand, bringing her to their side.

Virginia studied Walt. He looked even more handsome in his Sunday best, even if he did look a little uncomfortable.

"Who gives these women away?" the preacher said, bringing her back to the present.

The deputy studied the group, then smiled. "I do," he said, then stepped back.

The preacher did a magnificent job, and the service was very moving. Agreeing to a double wedding was the best thing they could have done. Warmth spread through Virginia as each couple repeated their vows, and each groom placed a wedding ring on their bride's finger.

"I now declare you husband and wife," the preacher declared, his hands taking in all four newlyweds standing before him. "You may now kiss your brides."

Walt turned to Virginia and grinned. He pulled her close, cupped her face, then kissed her deeply. She leaned into him. Never had she felt so drawn to another person the way she had to Walt. Knowing they would spend the rest of their lives together was very special, and she looked forward to the years to come.

The only accommodation available in town was either the saloon or the boarding house.

Both couples had decided spending their wedding night at the boarding house was a better option. After all, who in their right mind would want to spend time at the saloon? Walt had broken up far too many fights there to feel comfortable.

They had opted not to have a big wedding feast, but invited a small group of friends back to the boarding house. All the ladies had pitched in the day before to help with the cooking, making it far easier for Annie.

The three boarders had decorated the buggies sometime between the brides arriving and the couples stepping outside the church. The words *Just Married* trailing behind. It seemed silly for such a short distance, but the grooms wanted the day to be special for their brides.

Virginia

Both couples arrived back at the boarding house, and Walt helped his bride down from the buggy. His hands outstretched, he placed them around her waist. A shiver went through him. "I can't believe you are finally Mrs. Walton Riley," he said, shaking his head as he lifted her down.

"You better believe it," she said with a smile. "I can't wait to spend the rest of my life with you."

"I love you more than life itself," he whispered against her ear. Then carried her across the threshold.

Epilogue

Six years later…

Walt stared down into the face of his youngest son.

Victor, their firstborn, was five, and his little sister, Myra, was three. The latest baby, Wesley, was five months old. He already recognized his father, which sent a thrill down Walt's spine. He chucked the boy under the chin, then pulled him close. "I still find it hard to believe I'm a father again," he told Virginia.

She smiled at him, setting his heart ablaze. "You better believe it. There's no way I could do this on my own." She held out her arms for the baby, who needed a diaper change. "You could do this if you'd prefer – it might make you realize you really *are* a father." She laughed then. Suddenly, a pungent odor filled the room, and Walt became even more determined to hand the baby over.

He went to the window that overlooked their property. After living in the marshal's quarters for a few months, then discovering Virginia was with child, they thought harder about their future. As a single man, Walt could happily live out his days as a marshal. As a family man, it wasn't ideal.

Virginia

Instead, they pooled their money and bought a small property on the outskirts of Shady Hollow. It had everything they would ever need. There were three bedrooms, which would accommodate a growing family, an established vegetable garden, and a well close to their home.

Their horse breeding business provided a steady income; more than enough to keep them happy. As marshal at the time, Walt was one of the first to hear about the ranch going on the market when the previous owner died. As sad as it was, it was the best thing Walt could have done for his family.

"Papa," Victor said, running up to his father. "I thought we were riding today." The boy was already a splendid rider, and even at three, so was Myra.

Walt was proud of their achievements – in these past few years, they'd built the run down ranch into a profitable business. They sold their quality horses locally and had ranchers travel from far away to buy their stock. He earned enough with the property to employ two cowboys, and the way things were going, he'd have to employ more soon.

Apart from the fact Virginia had been traumatized on her arrival in Shady Hollow, he could not regret the events of that day. Without them, they would never have met.

"Come on, Victor," he said, his hand reaching out to the boy. "Let's saddle the pony." A smile lit up his son's face.

"Me too, Papa!" Myra shouted, running across the room. Walt glanced across to his wife. She nodded her accent.

"Let me put Wesley down for a nap, and then I can help." Myra jumped for joy and clapped her little hands. Her antics warmed his heart. As much as he had workers who could help teach the children to ride, he was their father, and wanted to spend as much time with them as he could. It was one of the deciding factors in giving up his job as a marshal.

Pete Nolan had always been a good deputy and was now a terrific marshal. His wife had not been averse to his promotion, since it came with a hefty pay rise. It helped they didn't have children.

The young family made their way to the stables. Walt lifted Victor onto a box he'd built to bring the child up to the right height to brush the pony he'd brought to teach his children to ride. If Victor wanted to do this, he had to learn there was hard work that came with it. At five, Walt's expectations were low, but he wanted his son to understand riding wasn't all fun. He watched proudly as Victor brushed the best way he could.

Virginia

Together, they added the saddle, although, in reality, Walt did all the work. He then swung his son up onto the pony's back.

He led the boy out onto the field and around in a circle. "My turn," Myra pleaded.

Walt grinned. "Soon. Give your brother time first."

Victor sat straight in the saddle. "Look at me, Mama." He grinned at her as they circled around again. When they stopped, Myra was quick to line up for her turn. Walt helped his son down, and Myra flung herself over the fence toward her father.

"Myra," Walt said, his gaze enough to stop the child in her tracks. "What have we said about jumping the fence?"

She hung her head low and pouted. "Can't do it when horses or the pony is there."

"Exactly. We don't want you to get trampled, now do we?"

"No, Papa." Moments later, she threw herself into her father's arms for him to place her on the saddle.

They were on their first walk around the field when Walt heard a wagon arriving.

Familiar voices had him smiling. Sherman and Annie Henderson had arrived for lunch as planned. Their three children were around the same age as the Riley children, and the young ones all enjoyed each other's company. The children ran to each other and wrapped their little arms around their friends in a big bear hug. Even Myra was rushing to get down off the pony and go to her friends.

Walt glanced about. This was the life he'd always wanted. He just didn't know it before. Until meeting Virginia, he believed his fate was that of a single man.

"I brought cake," Annie announced, handing the plate of food over to her dear friend. "Where's Wesley?" she asked, glancing about.

"He's napping. Poor boy was tired." Just then, they heard the baby crying. Virginia rushed into the house and returned soon afterwards, holding the baby.

"May I hold him?" Annie asked, holding her arms out to take Wesley. She breathed him in, smiling as she did. "I love the way babies smell. It makes me want another one," she said. "But Sherman says enough." She grinned then and leaned into Virginia and whispered conspiratorially, but her voice was loud enough for everyone to hear. "Too late." Her smile said it all.

Virginia smiled broadly. "Walt, there's something I've been meaning to tell you," she said, rubbing her belly.

Virginia

He stepped toward his wife and hugged her. "I love you so much," he whispered, instinctively knowing what she wanted to tell him, and not really caring if the others heard. He wanted the entire world to know how much he loved her, and would never stop telling her.

From the Author

Thank you so much for reading my book – I hope you enjoyed it.

I would greatly appreciate you leaving a review where you purchased, even if it is only a one-liner. It helps to have my books more visible!

~*~

About the Author

Multi-published, award-winning and bestselling author Cheryl Wright, former secretary, debt collector, account manager, writing coach, and shopping tour hostess, loves reading.

She writes both historical and contemporary western romance, as well as romantic suspense.

She lives in Melbourne, Australia, and is married with two adult children and has six grandchildren, and twin great-grandchildren.

When she's not writing, she can be found in her craft room making greeting cards.

Cheryl Wright

Links

Website: *http://www.cheryl-wright.com/*

Facebook Reader Group:
https://www.facebook.com/groups/cherylwrightauthor/

Join My Newsletter:

https://cheryl-wright.com/newsletter/
(and receive a free book)

Milton Keynes UK
Ingram Content Group UK Ltd.
UKHW021015110624
444053UK00014B/698

9 780648 640455

When Virginia Black accepted a position as a governess, she didn't expect it to end so abruptly. After being inadvertently compromised, she is banished before she even meets her charges.

Taking the next train out of town, she finds herself in yet another precarious situation.

Marshal Walton Riley is simply doing his job when he comes across the damsel in distress. He has no idea why, but is drawn to her. His work dictates his need to spend time with her, but after the dust settles, will he be able to keep away from the woman he's become so fond of?

cheryl-wright.com

ISBN 978-0-6486404-5-5